Our Lives, Our World

Japan

Chrysalis Education

Distributed in the United States by
Smart Apple Media
2140 Howard Drive West
North Mankato, Minnesota 56003

Photography copyright © Kaori Sato, Chikako Sugihara
and Yuichiro Matsuda, 2004

Compiled and edited by Susie Brooks
Editorial manager: Joyce Bentley
Designer: Keren-Orr Greenfeld
Photographic consultant: Jenny Matthews
Photographic coordinator: Chris Steele-Perkins
Picture researcher: Jamie Dikomite
Translator and consultant: Kyoko Gibbons

ISBN 1 59389 233 0

Library of Congress Control Number: 2004108814

Printed in China

10 9 8 7 6 5 4 3 2 1

The publishers would like to thank the photographers,
Kaori Sato, Chikako Sugihara, and Yuichiro Matsuda, for
capturing the lives of these wonderful children on film and
to Chris Steele-Perkins for his support and
encouragement.

Contents

Konnichiwa! — Hello!

We are the children of Japan and we can't wait to share our lives with you in this book!

Welcome to Japan!

We've got so much to show you! Let's start by telling you a little bit about our country. We hope you'll come and see Japan for yourself some time soon!

The country

Japan is in Eastern Asia. It is a narrow island country between the North Pacific Ocean and the Sea of Japan. Its nearest neighbors are North and South Korea, Russia, and China.

The capital city

Tokyo is the capital of Japan. It is one of the world's busiest cities.

Mountains

Mount Fuji is our highest and most famous mountain.

Land and climate

Japan is made up of four main islands and many tiny ones. Most of the country is covered with hills and mountains. The climate varies from North to South, but it is mainly hot and rainy during the summer and cooler in the winter.

The flag

This is our national flag. The red circle represents the sun.

Royal flower

The chrysanthemum flower is the symbol of our emperor and his family.

Speak Japanese!

konnichiwa—hello

sayonara—goodbye

dozo—please

domo arigato—thank you

Koichiro

Hi! I'm Koichiro Maeda and I am 7 years old. I live with my mom, dad, and brother in the town of Yokohama, not far from our capital city, Tokyo. My aunt and cousins live in the same apartment building—come and meet my family!

"My family are more important to me than anything else in the world!"

These aren't all my brothers and sisters! I have one brother, Yuya, who is 4. The others are my cousins. I play with Azusa every day.

I have my own room, but I like to sleep in my parents' bed, too. Mom is good at reading stories!

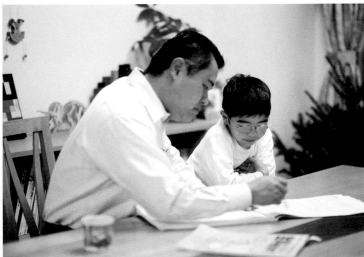

Dad makes sure I work hard on my school homework.

My school is next door to my house. There are 630 pupils there. We all meet for assembly at the beginning of the semester.

In the first lesson of the year, we write down our New Year's resolutions using a brush and ink. I write that I want to improve my goal keeping skills!

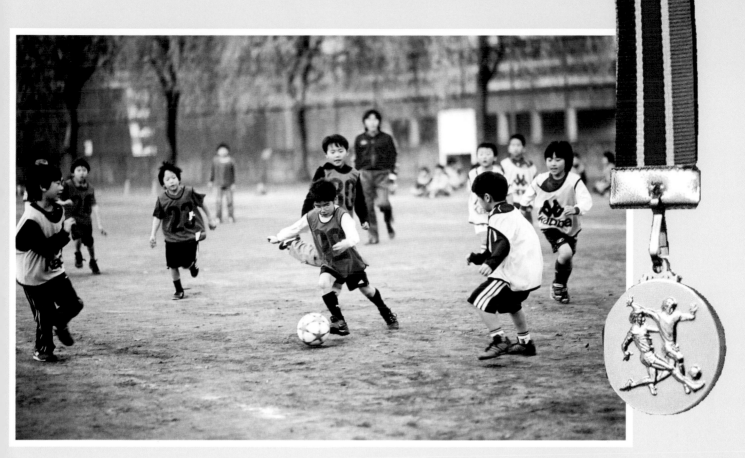

Soccer is my favorite subject and my hobby. I won this medal for being the best player in a game! One day I hope to be a professional soccer player.

In my spare time, I play video games with my best friend, Koki.

I'm good at skiing, too. I learned to ski almost as soon as I could walk! The mountains in Japan have lots of snow.

9

My grandparents live near Osaka in Southwest Japan. When I visit them, I have to travel by plane. Here I am getting lost at the airport!

Every year at my grandparents' house, we make rice cakes. You can see me eating one on page 6. We prepare them in the traditional way.

We cook a huge pot of steamed rice and put it in a big wooden tub.

We take turns to squash the rice with a mallet, adding water to make sticky dough.

We scoop out balls of the dough and shape them into cakes.

We use some of the cakes for decorations. The rest, we eat!

Sometimes my family take me to visit the grave of our ancestors. We put our hands together and close our eyes, while we quietly pray and think about the people who have died.

Remembering the dead

People in Japan traditionally visit their family tomb during the time of the equinoxes (March and September). There is also a yearly festival when the spirits of the dead are said to return to Earth. Relatives gather together and welcome the spirits home. At the end of the festival, paper lanterns are lit to guide the spirits back to their world.

Miyu

My name is Miyu Akeboshi. I am 8 years old and I live in Saitama, near Tokyo. Our home is on the second floor of an apartment building—it has a great view! My dad works a lot, so Mom looks after me and my 5-year-old brother, Atsuya.

"I am always laughing. I laugh too much when someone says something funny!"

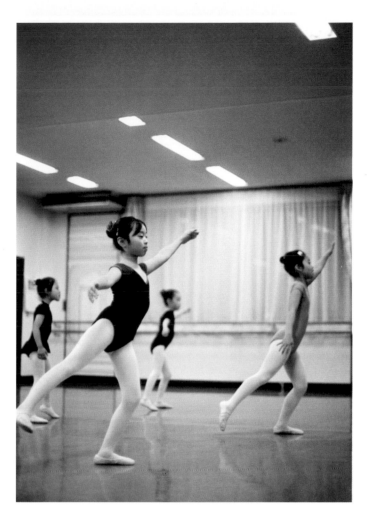

My best friend is Kurumi. We go to ballet lessons together twice a week.

I love listening to the gentle ballet music and focusing on my moves.

Dancing makes me hungry! I look forward to traditional meals like this one, when we eat foods such as fish, rolled omelette, sweet potato paste with chestnuts, noodle soup, and black beans.

Every day when I get to school I have to change from my outdoor shoes into indoor ones. Mom is taking me shopping for a new pair, because my feet have grown!

We also go to the supermarket. I help pick out the food I like!

My shopping list

noodles	✓
rice	✓
fruit	✓
eggs	✓
tofu	✓
tuna	✓
cod eggs	✓
soybeans	✓
seaweed	✓
soy sauce	✓
potato chips	✓
rice cakes	✓

On weekday mornings, I meet my friends outside my apartment and we walk to school together. It takes us about half an hour.

We all wear white safety helmets on our way to school.

There are 35 children in my class—some boys, some girls. We're in one of four classes in the second year. Our lessons run from 8:45 AM to 3:00 PM. We also get lots of homework!

Earthquakes

Japan is a country that suffers from a lot of earthquakes. Children are given earthquake drills at school, where they are taught to hide under their desks and hold onto their legs. Some schools also give pupils safety helmets. These may have the school logo on the front.

15

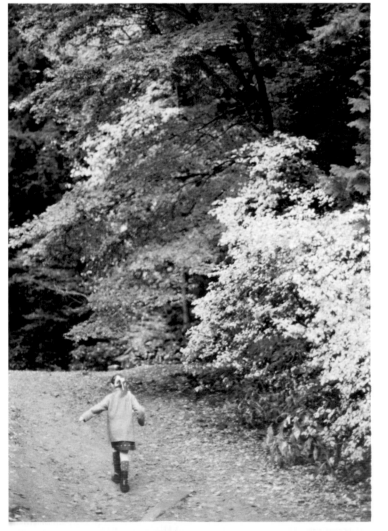

Sometimes I go with my family to pray at the shrine. It is pretty here, especially in the fall when the maple trees are brightly colored!

Religious beliefs

The Japanese are not generally strict about religion. But their traditions are often linked to Buddhism and an ancient faith called Shinto. The shrine is a Shinto place of worship. People usually visit shrines on special occasions, such as festivals.

At the shrine, we write wishes on the back of wooden prayer boards. I wish for the world to be full of smiles and laughter! The boards have a picture of an animal, related to the year we are in. I was born in 1995, the year of the boar!

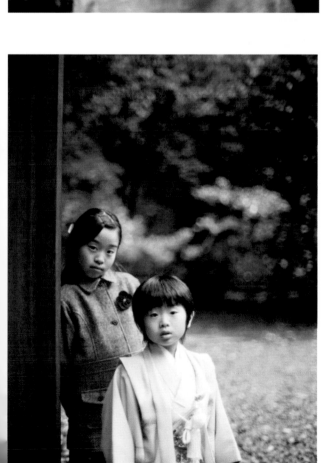

Atsuya is wearing a traditional Japanese gown called a kimono. It is made of silk and has a painting of an eagle on the back. He is dressed up for a special children's festival, where we give thanks for his good health and happiness.

Jiyu

Welcome to my home! I am Jiyu Ogami and I am 4. I have two older brothers—Hiroshi, who is 28, and Satoshi, who is 25. My mom and dad are farmers. We live in a log house that my dad built. It is on Hokkaido, Japan's north island.

"My name—Jiyu—means freedom."

The winters are very cold here. I like playing in the snowy fields and visiting the farm animals. The horses are my favorites—we have 50 of them!

At the farm, we have a restaurant and rooms for visitors to stay in. We train the horses for people to ride. There are also 300 beef cattle, 70 sheep, a dog, a cat, and lots of wild squirrels and birds.

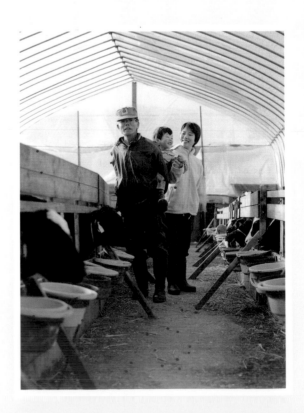

Every day my dad shifts hay on the tractor. Sometimes I go with him—I keep him awake when he's feeling sleepy! One day I might be a farmer myself—but I would rather be a soccer player!

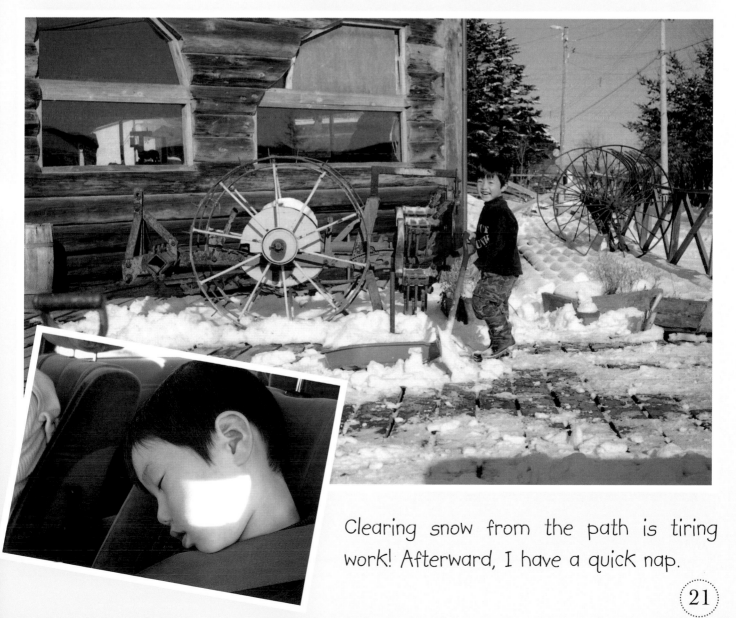

Clearing snow from the path is tiring work! Afterward, I have a quick nap.

This is my breakfast. I am having bread, milk, dried fruit with honey, Japanese cake, and tangerines. These are some of my favorite foods.

Japanese meals

Western-style food like Jiyu's is becoming more popular in Japan. But a traditional Japanese breakfast would include rice, soup, grilled fish, and pickles. A typical lunch or dinner dish is sushi—bite-size portions of rice, rolled with seafood or vegetables, and often wrapped in seaweed. In Japan, people eat with chopsticks instead of knives and forks.

I do not go to school yet, but I learn some things by watching videos in English. I like programs with cheerful music and laughter. Playing the piano makes me happy, too. So does the children's area in our local department store!

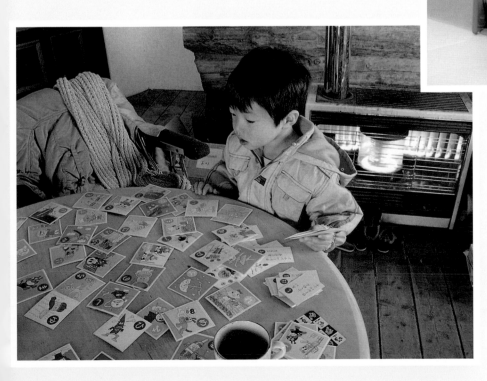

Here I am picking out picture cards in a game called "karuta". I love all the bright colors. I also like playing with toy tractors, cars, and building bricks.

23

Yui

Hello! My name is Yui Sato and I am 7 years old. I live in Fukushima with my parents, grandparents, and two little brothers—Ayumi, who's 5 and Nozomi, 2.

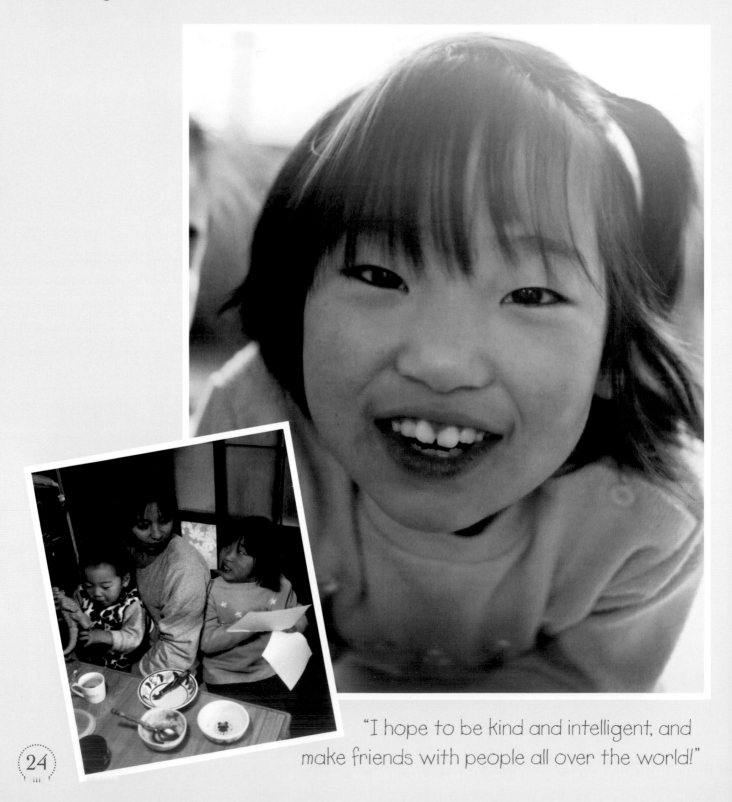

"I hope to be kind and intelligent, and make friends with people all over the world!"

Housing in Japan

Japan is a small country but it has a huge population. In most cities, people live in tall apartment buildings, because there is no space to build more houses. People with big homes like Yui's often share them with their grandparents.

Our house is very big compared to many homes in Japan. There are more than 10 rooms, but we only use six of them! In the picture below, I am closing the paper screen that divides our living room from the rest of the house.

Traditional rooms

People must take off their shoes when they enter a Japanese house. Many homes have a traditional room with straw mats—called tatami mats—on the floor. The mats may be sat on at mealtimes. Often there is a spare futon bed which can be rolled out at night and put away in the daytime. The traditional room has no windows and is separated from the hallway by a paper screen.

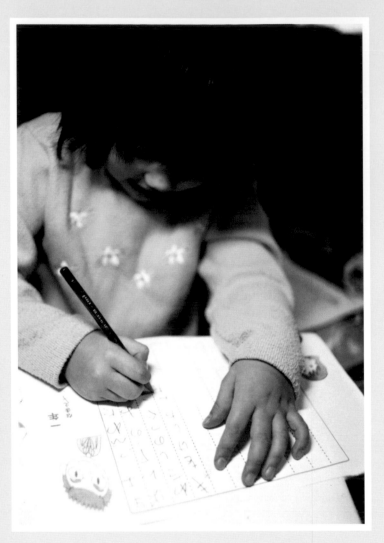

Kanji

The symbols that are used in traditional Japanese writing are called "kanji". Each one stands for a word or part of a word. There are many thousands of kanji. Children have to learn 1,006 of them by the end of their sixth year at school!

I like doing my homework in kanji. I'm writing a report to tell my teacher what I've done today and what has happened around me.

美り石は、8才の現在、自り
こを好んでいるようです。
しました 絵は、彼女が私
上げている「そのくん」という
されました 写真概季の 団報
などを集めると良い"と記述
自身の手から 作り出された物
、送付することに致しました
カ字も書かれていますし、デ
ンも良いのではないかと思
ナゆが集めている物（宝は
きなビー玉のような物だっ
写真no.18 参照）、送付
り断いたしました。

On Saturdays I go to piano lessons. Playing in my first piano concert was the most exciting thing I've ever done!

I spend a lot of time doing crafts, especially beadwork and knitting. My grandpa is an artist, so I sometimes draw pictures with him. My aunt made these straw flip-flops with painted flowers!

Here I am rolling some old newspaper to make an origami sword.

Origami

Origami is the traditional Japanese art of paper folding. Beautiful objects can be made by folding a sheet of paper in different ways, without using scissors or glue! Typical shapes are flowers, birds, butterflies, and other plants and animals.

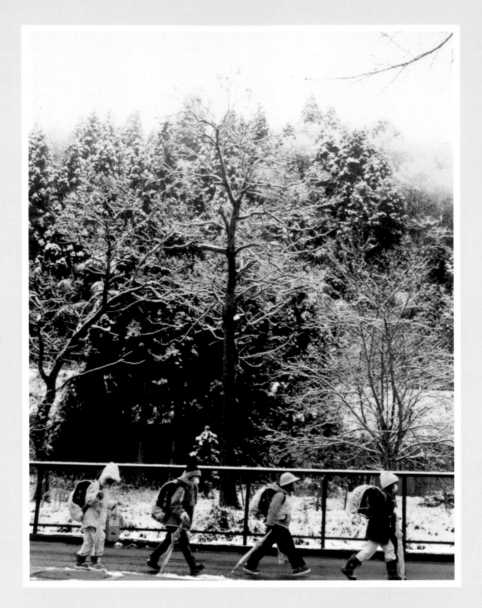

I walk to school with my friends. We carry our *books* in *backpacks*, and we need to dress in warm clothes in the snowy, winter weather.

Friendly Names

In Japan, the word "chan" is often tagged on the end of a girl's first name. It is a sign of fondness and is used mainly by close friends and relatives. In the same way, young boys are called "kun". For adults, it is polite to add "san" after their name.

These are some of my classmates: (from left to right) Hikaru-kun, Nodoka-chan, me, Akane-chan, Negumi-chan, Wakana-chan (my best friend), and Kasumi-chan.

On the weekends, I like to go into town. Fukushima is much smaller and quieter than Tokyo. This is the main street, outside my house. I am allowed to go out by myself, as long as I tell someone in my family where I'm going.

Traveling around

In Japan, the best way to travel from place to place is by train. There are various types of train, ranging from local ones, which stop at every station, to express trains that travel at high speed. The fastest are the bullet trains, called "shikansen", which travel 185 miles (300 kilometers) per hour! They have their own special tracks and platforms, and run only between the major stations.

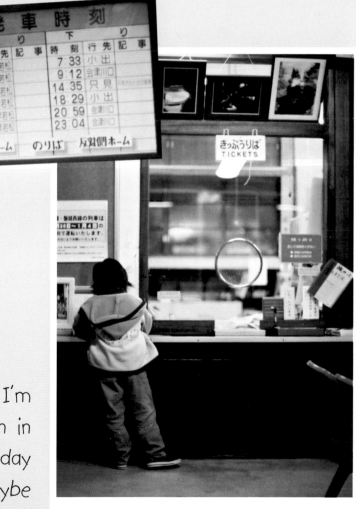

Here I am at our local train station. I'm checking the timetable, which is written in kanji. Traveling makes me excited—one day I hope to travel all around the world. Maybe I'll meet you somewhere!

Our Year

JANUARY

New Year's Day We visit shrines and temples, exchange cards, play games, and eat special foods.

FEBRUARY

Bean-scattering ceremony We celebrate the end of winter by scattering roasted soybeans!

Koichiro's birthday:
March 17th
Jiyu's birthday:
March 25th

MARCH

Girls' day We display beautiful dolls to celebrate the health and happiness of girls.
Spring equinox We visit family graves.

Spring school vacation: late March to early April

APRIL

Flower festival We have picnics and parties to welcome the flowering of the cherry blossom trees.

MAY/JUNE

Boys' day We fly streamers and display warrior dolls to celebrate the health and happiness of boys.

Miyu's birthday:
June 1st

JULY

Star festival We write wishes on paper streamers and hang them from bamboo branches, then pray for the wishes to come true.

Summer school vacation: late July to late August

AUGUST

Buddhist spirit festival We light lanterns and clean our houses to welcome the spirits of the dead home.

SEPTEMBER/OCTOBER

Autumn equinox We visit family graves.
Moon viewing We put out ornaments and food offerings to greet the fall moon.

Yui's birthday:
September 27th

NOVEMBER

7-5-3 festival Boys 5 and 3 years old, and girls 7 and 3 go to the shrine. They are blessed and given lucky bags of candy to wish them a long life.

DECEMBER

Christmas In Japan this is not a religious day, but we give each other presents and cards.
New Year's Eve We spend time cleaning our houses. As the year ends, the temple bells ring slowly, 108 times.

Winter school vacation:
late December to early January

Sayonara! — Goodbye!

Glossary

ancestor A relation who lived in years gone by.

Buddhism A world religion that is very popular in Asia.

emperor The ruler of Japan.

equinox A date when day and night are equal in length.

futon A roll-out mattress, used on the floor as a bed.

kanji The symbols used in Japanese writing.

kimono A traditional Japanese robe with wide sleeves, usually made of silk.

origami The art of folding paper to make ornaments.

Shinto An ancient Japanese religion.

shrine A place of worship.

sushi A traditional Japanese dish made up of bite-size portions of rice, seafood, and vegetables.

Index